How Elephants Lost their Wings

Retold by Lesley Sims

Designed and illustrated
by Katie Lovell

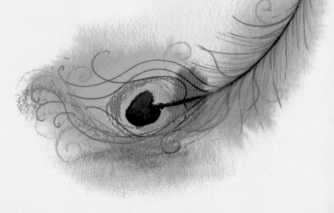

Reading Consultant: Alison Kelly
Roehampton University

This story is about flying elephants,

two gods,

houses,

peacocks

and
banana
trees.

3

Once upon a time,
elephants could fly.

They flew everywhere.

They flew high
into the sky...

and down to the ground.

They even
looped
the loop.

Sometimes, the gods
flew on their backs.

But the elephants
were noisy.

They yelled, and
crowed like roosters.

Trees and houses
shook below them.

ock-a-
doodle-
doo!

They flew into trees
and smashed them.

They landed on houses...

and fell
right through.

Soon all the trees were broken and there were no houses left.

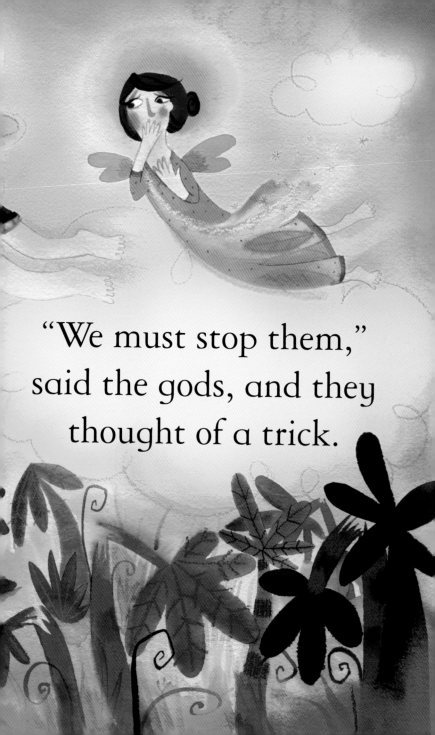

"We must stop them," said the gods, and they thought of a trick.

They invited the elephants to a grand feast. The elephants ate...

...and ate.

When their tummies
were full, they slept.

The gods took
away their wings.

They gave
them to the
peacocks

and the
banana
trees.

The elephants
were very cross.

They shouted
and they stomped.

But they didn't get
their wings back

and they never
flew again.

Puzzles
Puzzle 1

Find these things
in the picture:

elephant
trunk
houses
hill
tree
wings

Puzzle 2

Can you spot the differences between these two pictures? There are six to find.

Puzzle 3

Put the pictures in order.

A

B

C

D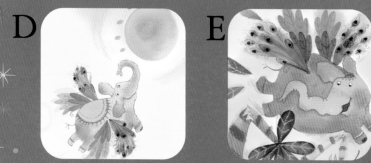

E

What happened next?

Puzzle 4

A

or

B?

Puzzle 5

A   or   B?

Answers to puzzles
Puzzle 1

wings

trunk

tree

houses

elephant

hill

Puzzle 2